WHAT IF THE
ZEBRAS
LOST THEIR
STRIPES?

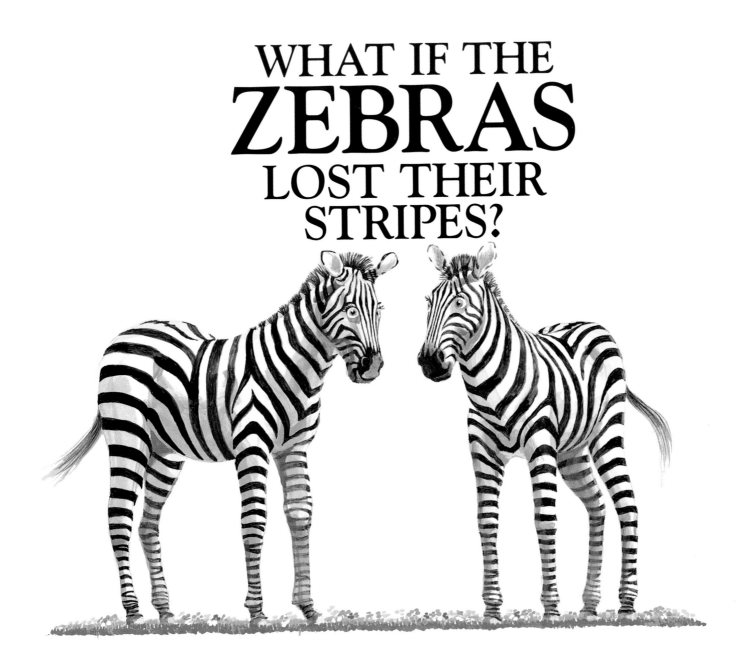

By JOHN REITANO
Illustrated by WILLIAM HAINES

Paulist Press
New York/Mahwah, N.J.

Jacket design by William Haines

Library of Congress Cataloging-in-Publication Data

Reitano, John.
    What if the zebras lost their stripes / by John Reitano ; illustrated by William
Haines.
        p.   cm.
    Summary: If the zebras lost their stripes and became different from one another,
some white and some black, would they turn and fight each other and stop living life
as loving friends?
    ISBN 0-8091-6649-6
    [1. Zebras—Fiction. 2. Prejudices—Fiction. 3. Stories in rhyme.] I. Haines,
William, ill. II. Title.
PZ8.3.R284Wh   1998
[E]—dc21
                                                                            98-14643
                                                                              CIP
                                                                              AC

Published by Paulist Press
997 Macarthur Boulevard
Mahwah, New Jersey 07430

Printed and bound in Mexico

To Jennie and Frank Reitano,
who taught me to see with my heart.
– JR

To my wonderful daughters Debbie, Cindy,
Shelly and Vicki with love.
– WH

Special thanks to our editor, Karen Scialabba,
for bringing the Zebras to life.

What if the Zebras

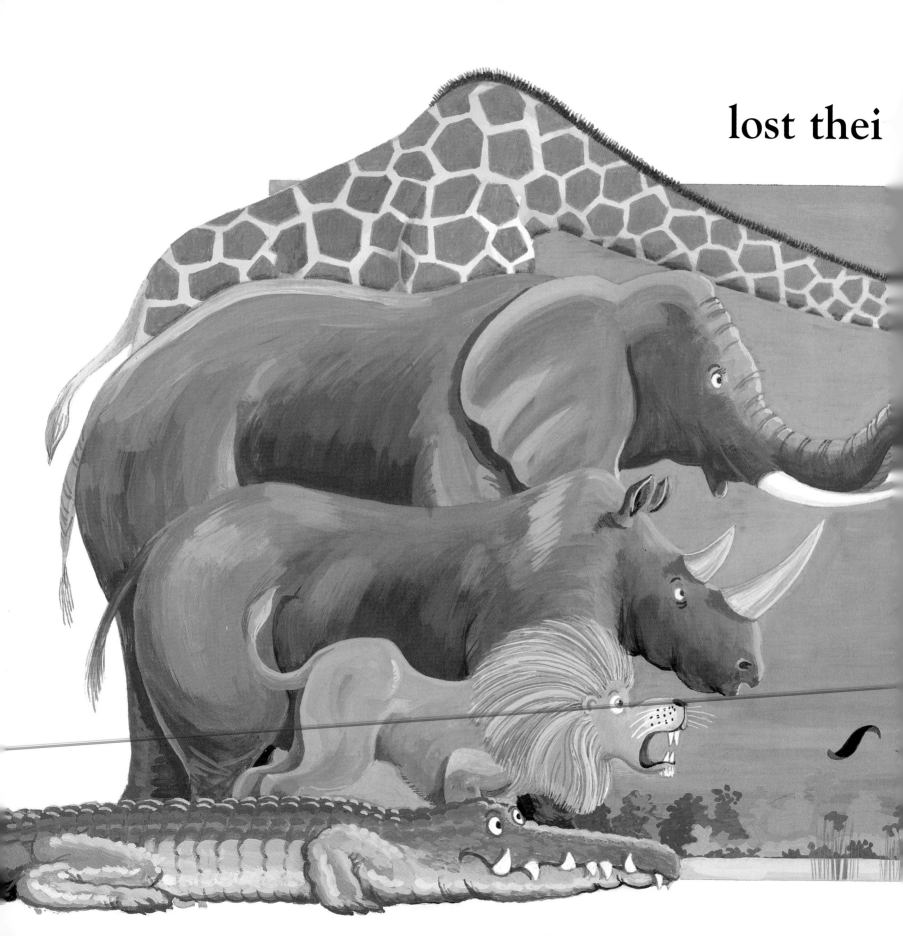

lost thei

tripes, and some lost black

and some lost white?

Would they think

hat it's all right,

Or would the Zebras

start to fight?

If the Zebras lost their stripes?

Would different colors be the end

Of living life as loving friends?

Would Zebras see themselves as Zebras?

Or would their colors make them start

To only see the ☾ black or white —

And not what lives within their hearts?

Would there be

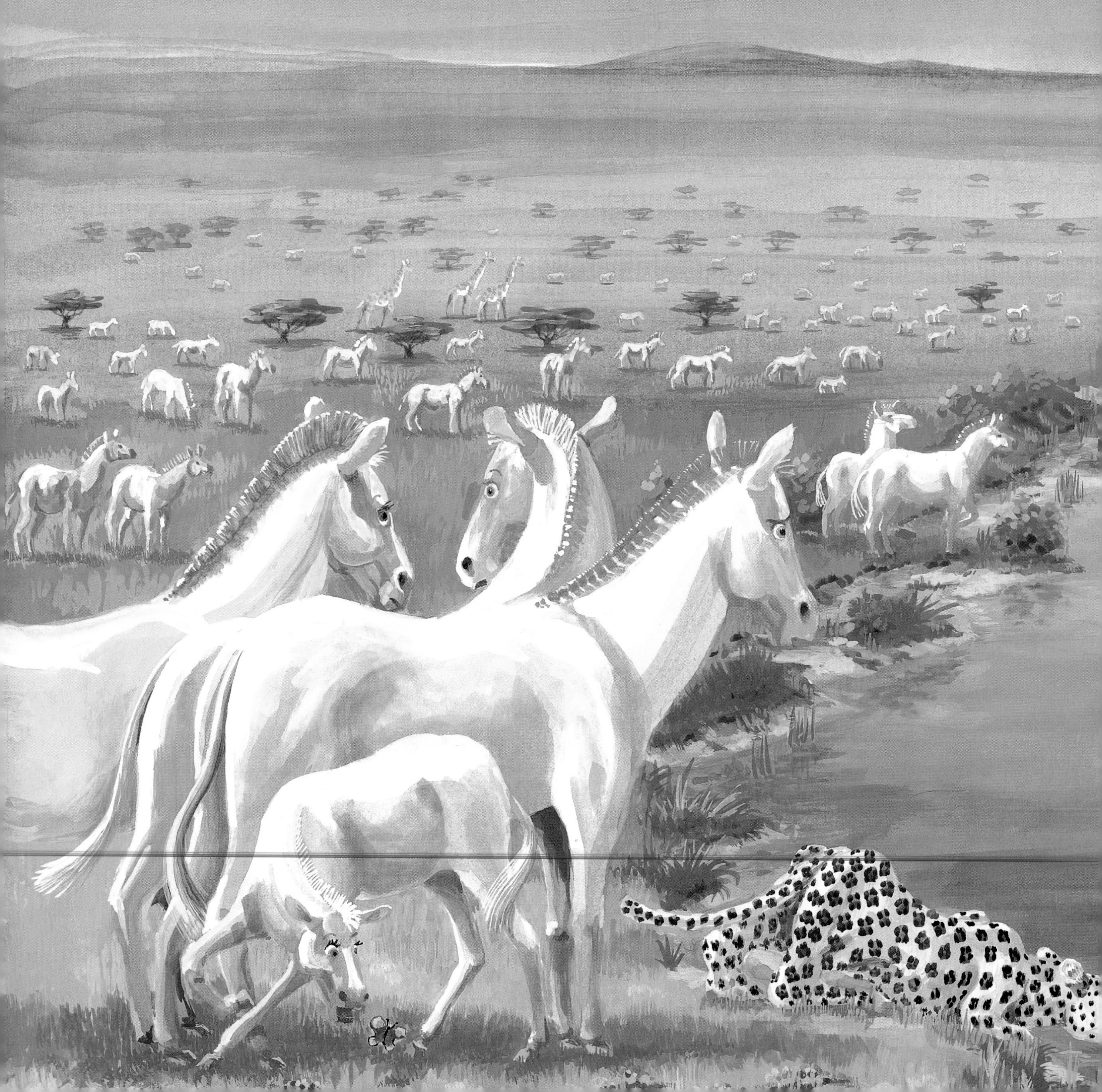

Could black

and white friends still hold hands?

Would Zebra children be okay

To join together, laugh and play?

I know why God gave Zebras stripes –

So that there'd be no black or white!

But, Zebras would be much too smart

To let their colors tear them apart!